T0208038

T'was the Night Before Fifth Grade

T'was the Night Before Fifth Grade

written by

Jeff Lisy

Illustrated by Abraham Lee

T'was the Night Before Fifth Grade

iUniverse books may be ordered through booksellers or by contacting:

iUniverse
1663 Liberty Drive
Bloomington, IN 47403
www.iuniverse.com
1-800-Authors (1-800-288-4677)

Because of the dynamic nature of the Internet, any web addresses or links contained in this book may have changed since publication and may no longer be valid. The views expressed in this work are solely those of the author and do not necessarily reflect the views of the publisher, and the publisher hereby disclaims any responsibility for them.

Any people depicted in stock imagery provided by Thinkstock are models, and such images are being used for illustrative purposes only. Certain stock imagery © Thinkstock.

ISBN: 978-1-4917-6801-3 (sc)
ISBN: 978-1-4917-6802-0 (e)

Library of Congress Control Number: 2015907394

Print information available on the last page.

iUniverse rev. date: 05/28/2015

This wonderful book belongs to:

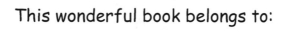

To my loving wife, Joanne; my children, John and Grace; and all my fifth-grade students.

'Twas the night before fifth grade. Alarm clocks were set.

All the kids were as snug as a bug in their beds.

Pencils and paper and rulers too would be going to school like cool boys and girls do.

Kids set out their clothes and lunches too. Backpacks were hung by the front door with care.

The kids nestled all warm in their beds while visions of numbers and letters danced in their heads.

But one fifth-grade boy was still wide-awake. He worried about fifth grade and the work he might get.

His stomach hurt, though he did not know why. He hid behind his locker. He was feeling quite shy.

"Hey there, John!" said Mr. Lisy.

He greeted each student by name.

"Huddle up, and we will play the name game."

Kids did arithmetic and reading—they loved their lunchtime too!

Then everyone listened to a story and did a special rhyme.

They dressed up in drama class from the costume closet.

"Look at me—I am Justin Timberlake!"

"And I'm Ariana Grande!"

But John just watched the other students as they did their classwork. At his desk by himself is right where he stayed.

He drew a number line as big as a tree. He showed it to Mr. Lisy.

"That is an outstanding job! Keep it up!"

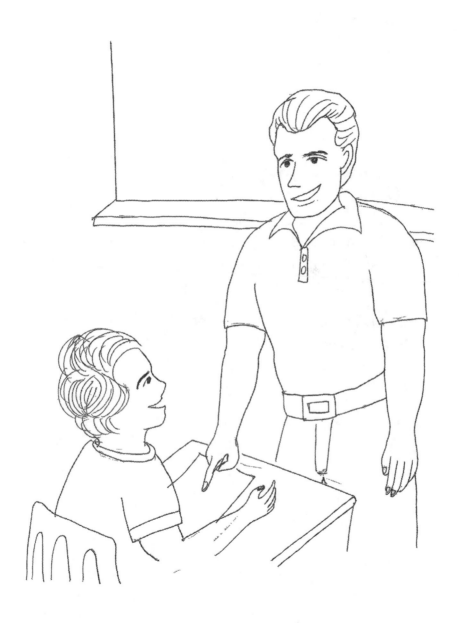

Then the students cleaned up their pencils and paper. They took a trip to the bathroom—one for the girls and one for the boys.

It was time for lunch, but John said, "No, thanks" and pushed his aside.

Then off they marched to recess time.

There were monkey bars to climb back and forth, a field to play soccer in, and swings to swing on.

After changing their shoes and hanging up their jackets, they gathered pencils and paper for their writer's workshop stories.

The kids buried their heads into their writing; soon there wasn't a peep. All was quiet—except for John, who couldn't think.

"I can't write without my pencil, Mr. Lisy. But I don't have it here!" cried out John.

When what to his upset eyes should appear but a big yellow pencil with a pink eraser on the end.

"It's okay," a little girl said. "Here—take mine."

"Thank you so very much," John said as he started to write the title of his story.

And just like that, he started writing his story in a snap!

After writer's workshop was over, he did his research paper with Grace.

"I'll look up information on dogs," said John.

"And I'll look up information on frogs."

When out in the hallway there arose such a clatter.

All the kids sprang to the classroom door to see what was the matter.

The principal rushed in wanting to tell the kids that their first day of fifth grade was over. "Have a great day, and I will see you tomorrow," said Principal Clover.

"See you tomorrow," said Mr. Lisy.

Wow! The first day was done.

"I'll be back!" John shouted. "Fifth grade is fun!"

The End

About the Author

Jeff Lisy was born in Des Plaines, Illinois. As a kid, he loved to play baseball and hang out with his friends.

He received his bachelor's degree in education from Northeastern Illinois University and his master's in curriculum and instruction from Concordia University.

He has spent the last fifteen years teaching at North Elementary School.

Jeff is the recipient of the 2015 Lighthouse Award for School District 62.

He lives with his wife, Joanne, and two children, John and Grace.

Jeff loves spending time with his family, going to his son's hockey games and his daughter's dance, and just playing outside.

About the Illustrator

Abraham J. Lee is a National Board-certified art teacher who currently teaches art at North Elementary School in Des Plaines, Illinois. He is a former regional vice president of Illinois Art Education Association and facilitated professional development workshops for art teachers in the greater Chicago area by establishing partnerships with art museums and educational institutions.

He is a recipient of 2007 Power of Art award presented by the Robert Rauschenberg Foundation and the Lab School of Washington, DC.

Mr. Lee received his BFA in art education from the University of Illinois at Urbana-Champaign in 1999 and his MEd in educational administration and supervision from Loyola University Chicago in 2005.

AUTOGRAPHS!

AUTOGRAPHS!

Me and My Friends

Printed in the United States
By Bookmasters